The 12 Days of Preschool

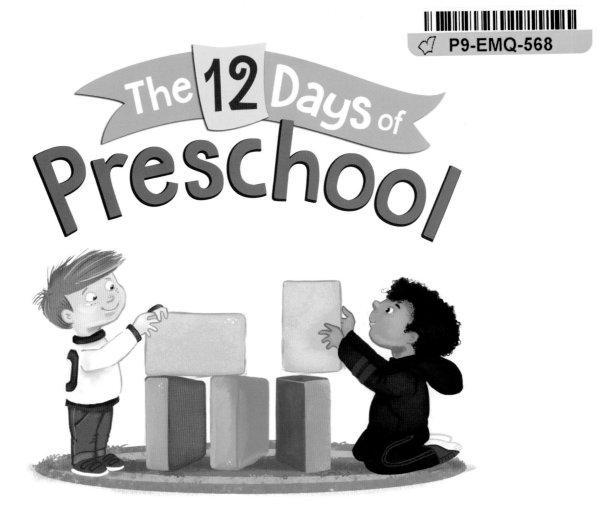

by Jenna Lettice • illustrated by Colleen Madden

A Random House PICTUREBACK® Book

Random House New York

Text copyright © 2018 by Jenna Lettice. Cover art and interior illustrations copyright © 2018 by Colleen Madden.
All rights reserved. Published in the United States by Random House Children's Books, a division of
Penguin Random House LLC, 1745 Broadway, New York, NY 10019. Pictureback, Random House,
and the Random House colophon are registered trademarks of Penguin Random House LLC.
rhcbooks.com
Library of Congress Control Number: 2017018719
ISBN 978-1-5247-6660-3 (trade) — ISBN 978-1-5247-6661-0 (ebook)
MANUFACTURED IN CHINA 10 9 8 7 6 5 4 3 2 1

On the **first** day of preschool,
we all learned how to share:

Our most favorite
fuzzy teddy bear.

On the **second** day of preschool,
we all learned how to share:

Two choo-choo trains
and our most favorite
fuzzy teddy bear.

On the third day of preschool,
we all learned how to share:

Three blue trikes,
Two choo-choo trains,
and our most favorite
fuzzy teddy bear.

STOP!

GO!

SLOW!

On the **fourth** day of preschool,
we all learned how to share:

Four finger paints,
Three blue trikes,
Two choo-choo trains,
and our most favorite
fuzzy teddy bear.

blue

red

On the **fifth** day of preschool,
we all learned how to share:

Five dinosaurs!
Four finger paints,
Three blue trikes,
Two choo-choo trains,
and our most favorite
fuzzy teddy bear.

On the **sixth** day of preschool,
we all learned how to share:

Six swings for swinging,
Five dinosaurs!

Four finger paints,
Three blue trikes,
Two choo-choo trains,
and our most favorite
fuzzy teddy bear.

On the **seventh** day of preschool,
we all learned how to share:

Seven snacks for munching,
Six swings for swinging,
Five dinosaurs!
Four finger paints,
Three blue trikes,
Two choo-choo trains,
and our most favorite
fuzzy teddy bear.

On the **eighth** day of preschool,
we all learned how to share:

Eight books for reading,
Seven snacks for munching,

Six swings for swinging,
Five dinosaurs!
Four finger paints,
Three blue trikes,
Two choo-choo trains,
and our most favorite
fuzzy teddy bear.

On the **ninth** day of preschool,
we all learned how to share:

Nine cots for sleeping,
Eight books for reading,
Seven snacks for munching,
Six swings for swinging,
Five dinosaurs!
Four finger paints,
Three blue trikes,
Two choo-choo trains,
and our most favorite
fuzzy teddy bear.

On the **tenth** day of preschool,
we all learned how to share:

Ten blocks for building,
Nine cots for sleeping,
Eight books for reading,
Seven snacks for munching,

Six swings for swinging,
Five dinosaurs!
Four finger paints,
Three blue trikes,
Two choo-choo trains,
and our most favorite
fuzzy teddy bear.

On the **eleventh** day of preschool,
we all learned how to share:

Eleven drums for banging,
Ten blocks for building,
Nine cots for sleeping,
Eight books for reading,
Seven snacks for munching,
Six swings for swinging,
Five dinosaurs!
Four finger paints,
Three blue trikes,
Two choo-choo trains,
and our most favorite
fuzzy teddy bear.

On the **twelfth** day of preschool,
we all learned how to share:

Twelve squares for hopping,
Eleven drums for banging,
Ten blocks for building,
Nine cots for sleeping,
Eight books for reading,
Seven snacks for munching,
Six swings for swinging,
Five dinosaurs!
Four finger paints,
Three blue trikes,
Two choo-choo trains . . .

. . . and our most favorite fuzzy teddy bear.

Welcome to preschool!